GW00725527

POETRY, PROSE & PEACE

An anthology of poems and short stories written during lockdown for the age of Coronavirus

To Christine with Love + thanks, from M.S.Walker 12/12/20 Enjoy!

Dr Tariq Shabbeer

edited by James Giles

Kingston Enquirer Media Limited
53 South Park Grove, New Malden, KT3 5DA
www.kingstonenquirer.co.uk

1 2 3 4 5 6 7 8 9 0

I would like to dedicate this work to my wife Nighat Taimuri, and sons Isa and Adam. And to all those who have died and suffered from this tragic crisis.

CONTENTS

ACKNOWLEDGMENTS

I am indebted to my long suffering
Mother, father, wife and sons
Without whose gigantic patience
I would not have begun
This epic narration of what I've done
In my small life under the sun
And I thank Save the World Club and James Giles,
KEC and all those good people,
Who helped me smile.

An Introduction

It seems I've become a lockdown singer and poet,
I was good before,
But did not know it.
Not a great Shakespeare,
Just your humble T. Shabbeer.

Finding simple rhymes to express,
More to you, by saying less,
For those like me,
With short attention,
It's much easier for,
Retention.

Lockdown Night

By the light of the dawning sun,
Which sheds its veil,
To the Eastern skies,
When the bees were busy,
And the winds and rains subsides.

As the morning chorus drowns,
Lockdown night's silence,
There's more to be explained,
That's known by science.

Fifteen weeks plus in isolation,
Was not as much a desolation,
When neighbours, friends and Council too,
Helped us cope and make do.
The world may burn and pillage,
But we are first, a 'Global Village'.

It didn't matter,
If you were, black or white,
The virus didn't care,
If you were, left or right,
We all united in the fight,

With our glorious NHS,
As our guiding light.

Korean, Arab, Turk or Greek,
A healthy world is all we seek.

For those who'll leave and travel far,
Don't forget just who you are,
Having lived or worked in KT3,
Be very proud of it, like me!
And as the twilight,
Creeps into the West,
I know I'm living, with the best,
Most kind, most generous, generally,
We all live here, happily.

So no matter where I roam,
I will never be, lost or alone.

And as the setting sun hangs low,
I'll remember and I'll know,
That New Malden,
The 'Honey' Coombes and
England
Is my home.

Clinicians and Physicians are Magicians

At noon, I got a splinter,
In my right hand index finger,
From a spiky Cactus plant.

Most of it came out,
With some grunts and little shouts,
But the needles went in deep,
And dig it out, I can't.

I thought, "I won't worry any doctor,
Or the A and E,
With such a minor thing,
I'll just look after me,
With some natural remedies."

I thought, "Block out all the pain,
When it dominates my brain,
There are so many sicker people,
So I mustn't be so vain"

Then that evening,
As I was gazing at the stars,
Wondering who we are,
I felt a little sting,
Though I didn't think a thing.

It hovered up and mocked me,
With a belly of my blood,
The 'mosquito' thing was ugly,
And flew off on to mud.

It took some time,
To see the tell-tail signs,
Of two 'vampire-like bites',
Across the left nape of my neck.

So on the seventh morning,
Waking from a pleasant snoring,
While stretching and a yawning,
I viewed it in the mirror groaning,
"What the heck?!".

The bite had got infected,
Now as big as fifty pee (50p).

Red and raw and painful,
I exclaimed,

"Someone please help me!"

So I gave the doc a ring,
And said, "I've had some type of sting",
They saw my close up photos,
Of the swelling like volcano,
And prescribed some medicine.

The penicillin worked,
Now it doesn't really hurt,

And I'm feeling pretty fine.

So don't you wait as long,
If something does go wrong,
See an NHS physician,
Who are the REAL magicians,
And check it out in time.

Birthday Poem

dedicated to Des Kay, Founder of Save the World Club

It was Des Kay's birthday,
So I wrote a poem,
On how I'm really glad,
To say I know him.

Chair of Save the World Club,
He rescues food,
He's Superman and
Santa Claus,
And he's never rude.

Light in heart,
He's having fun,
He's always joking,
And making puns.

He says,
'Every day's Christmas,
Doing things you like'.

'The Save the World Club charity
is here,
When bad times strike'.

So Happy Birthday,
Desmond Kay,

I hope you stay,
The same sweet way.

That is all,
I have to say,
I'll see you,
Another day.

A Loving Lockdown

By the nib of my pen,
Let me tell you my friend,
About our joyous thirtieth anniversary.
She's lit up my life,
Though I've given her strife,
Yet she's so complimentary.

She's more than I think,
And if the seas were all ink,
I could never describe,
Her beautiful eyes,
Or how we perfectly link.

If I owned rivers that flowed,
With diamonds and gold,
It wouldn't compare,
To the mother who's cared,
For all the love that we hold.

I scoured the world,
For diamonds and pearl's,
To show my love for you,
But jewels may crumble apart,
Next to your beautiful heart,
And all the things that you do.

So, by the ink of my pen,

It's my love that I send,
With this poem of,
Rapture for you.

If I captured the moon,
Or the Sun from the noon,
It wouldn't,
Compare with you.

Maytime Blooming

Vibrant poppies flame in majesty,
The sun revealing their mysteries,
What a gorgeous sight to see,
There is more to life than me.

Tomatoes, beans, kale and thyme,
Basil, mint and chive taste fine,
Coriander, onions, peppers, chillies,
Apples, pears, figs and lillies.

Sunflowers and teasels getting tall,
As pansies bloom and violas fall,
Grapes and lavender and lemon balm,
Scent the air to keep me calm.

Robins winging, blackbirds singing,
Pigeons swooping, squirrels digging,
And Admiral butterflies visit too,
With Painted Ladies, Cabbage Whites and Meadow Blues.

Summers' fruits will come your way,
If there's soil and light and water in the day,
Gardening will be your health and saviour,
When you enjoy these natural flavours.

Lockdown Daisies

Lock down daisies blooming there,
Like you haven't got a care,
Why do you flower?

Even in the darkest hour,
Glowing 'neath the new sunlight,
Colours made more vibrant bright.

Who are you calling to make a seed?

What will you give or receive?

Mysterious nature sing your song,
As Summers' days grow long,
The sun will rise and the sun will set,
But daisy chains will be here yet.

The Two metre-o-meter
Written in Week 13 of the Spring/Summer UK lockdown

Today they're debating,
And I'm anticipating,
Just what the experts might do.

They could loosen the rules,
But we shouldn't be fools,
'Cause we don't want,
A Covid Wave Two.

So I wouldn't lie,
When I say that I've tried,
A one point five (1.5) meterometer,
As a common denominator,
Between one meter and two.

Testing one meter I found,
That I didn't feel sound,
If I'm honest and true.

Whereas the two meterometer's,
Been like a thermometer,
For judging distance,
'Tween me and you.

It's hard to visualise,
Two meters in size,

A radius in which,
You can't meet.

That's four meters width,
Or thirteen (13) feet wide,
Or one hundred and thirty five (135),
Square feet.

I still long for an App,
That simply re-acts,
And isn't too verbose.

Like a car's proximity sensor,
With a human detector,
When others come too close.

So use your 'internal - ometer',
As your barometer,
If you really,
Have to go about.

But better yet still,
Is to have a strong will,
And stay inside,
Not out.

Mathematical Comparisons

for the two metre-o-meter!

The area of a four meter diameter (two meter radius) circle is:

- 12.566   square meters; or
- 135.26   square feet

The circumference of a 4 meter wide circle is over 41 feet.

.....

The area of a three meter diameter (1.5 meter radius) circle is:

- 7.07 square meters; or
- 76.09 square feet

The circumference of a 3 metre wide circle is 30.92 feet.

.....

The area of a two meter diameter (one meter radius) circle is:
- 3.146 square meters; or
- 33.82 square feet

The circumference of a 2 metre wide circle is 20.61 feet.

Summer's Coming

Summer's coming,
Bring the sun in,
Bees are humming,
Find the fun in,

Caring for your kin and kids,
Locking down to fight Covid,
Nature doesn't care,
You will find it there,
Waiting.

Air is sweeter,
Trees are greener,
Flowers bursting,
Heroes nursing,

Heaven bless the NHS,
We wish you all the very best,
Nature doesn't care,
You will find it there,
For you.
Warmth is coming,
Winds are passing,
Earth is warming,
Bees are swarming,

The Summer Sun,

Is on it's way,
The stormy clouds,
Will blow away,
Nature doesn't care,
You will find it there,
With you.

With you,
Peace be with you.

Sleepless Slumbers

12th August 2020

On the twelfth of August,
To be precise.
I was constantly turning,
Like my linen sheets were burning,
With my brain frying like an egg,
Like I was sleeping on a lava bed.

"Go to sleep", I said,
But those hell-hot thoughts,
Circulated round,
My sleepy head.

I counted sheep,
In the heat,
'Till they were,
All accounted for.

I counted backwards,
From a million,
'Till I just got so bored.
But, still my mind wouldn't rest,
Like it was on an endurance test.

Indeed, there is enough,
To make me sob,
Finding and staying in a job,

Worried 'bout my health,
My dwindling wealth ...
And though these times do sting,
I smile as if it doesn't mean a thing,
For I have faith in the,
Bigger scheme of things.

So I wrote these words,
So you can,
Say you heard,
What I've tried to sleep,
It's rather sad and makes me weep,
But you may suggest some other cures,
May be a mallet!
Or some liqueurs?

Because it's like there's no escape,
When I'm surrounded by,
That invasive oppressive heat I hate.

It's relentlessly there,
I'd die for some cold air,
I don't want to be warm,
Where are those,
Summer storms?

So, on a Sleepless Slumber,
Let me float off,
And go on under,
With a heaven-like,
Enchanted dream,
Where I can ponder,
What it means,
And share it,

In the morning,
With the family
As they are yawning.

Our sleepless dreams,
Weave tapestries of people and places,
Moulding the present with memories,
Long gone and past.

Is it not strange to you,
When good or bad dreams,
Come true?
'And those who,
Laugh out first,
Will no doubt,
Laugh the last.'

It's Harvest Time

It's Harvest Time,
I'm feeling fine.

Darkest blackcurrants bursting bright,
Like the deepest moon-less night,
Scrumptious strawberries sweet and ripe,
Luscious loganberries crimson light.

Parsley, sage, rosemary, thyme,
Basil, mint and beans taste fine,
Coriander, mustard, oregano, chillies,
Apples, pears, figs and lilies.

Feed the world with cucumber soup,
Tomatoes, potatoes and kiwi fruit,
Snow drops, daffodils and tulips root,
Geraniums, chrysanthemum and
nasturtiums shoot.

Sunflowers and teasels standing tall,
Cascading pansies and violas fall,
Grapes and lavender and lemon balm,
Scent the air and keep you calm.

Red currants, rhubarb, leek and bay,
Growing strong while foxes play,
Birds and bees come a flocking,

While Kingston Green Radio keeps a rocking.

Robins winging, blackbirds singing,
Pigeons swooping, squirrels digging,
And Admiral butterflies visit too,
With Painted Ladies, Cabbage Whites and Meadow Blues.

From cacti to seeds,
And fungi to trees,
The Kingston Environment Centre,
Has all that you need.

Summers' fruits have come and gone,
Preserved in dreams and poems and song,
So recall the joy of natural flavours,
And plant next Spring for future saviours.

The Damson Spirit

On a stormy Sunday dark and dreary
When you may be feeling weary
I'd like to share my true story
That's really one of hope and glory

I met a damson spirit
Who put his whole heart in it
And helped me pick a pound or two
For his daughter he called Sue

I said, "Are you really real?"
I can't see you but feel
That you are really there
And it's for your daughter that you care

So we picked along some time
And we got along real fine
He said, "Tell my daughter, I love her"
And I'm picking damsons above her

So I drove to Sue with plums,
To make jam of damsons,
Then I tactfully said,
That a spirit spoke in my head…

So she thought a little bit
And she nearly had to sit

Cause her father'd passed on
And loved picking damsons

He'd taught her how to cook
Living by the book
So finally she said
"I'll talk to him in prayers by my bed"
"And ask him what he said"

So I thought to myself, "That's weird"
Cause it's nothing to be feared
Infact it's rather fantastic
That it made me feel euphoric
For the Damson Spirit's fine
And we'll all join him in time.

Thoughts remained inside my head
As I spun around in bed
For every night at Three Twenty One (3.21 am)
The damson spirit came and sung
A song he said he liked in life
He said it was the words he liked
Called 'Open Your Heart' to me by Madonna

I said, 'Even though it's very nice to meet you
And it is a pleasure and an honour to greet you
Can't you see that I'm in bed?
And he said, "Well that's exactly when I'll come
When your drowsy dreams form in your head"

He said, "So few believe that you hear me
So find your way to the Methuselah tree
And I'll take you to the year
Three thousand and twenty three"

I said, "I don't believe you"
But I'll come along to see
Because I trust in God and I don't fear you

So he said, "Follow the winding path to the old oak tree
Past the apple on the path and the honey bees
Then touch the oak tree's bark
Hug it's wrinkled trunk so dark
Press you ear against the tree
And hear which way the water flows to me"

So on October the seventh I ventured there
Through the thickets without a fear
Past the bee hives and the apple lying there
Finding that Timeless Oak Tree the spirit came to me
Stating, "An oak takes three hundred years to grow
Three hundred years to live
And three hundred years to die"
"Hear which way the water runs
And learn the reasons why"

By the light of the Halloween moon
I am so happy to be back so soon
To tell you that I was transported forward
By over one thousand years
Through different time dimensions
With a helpless morbid fear

My head was spinning
As the light was dimming
When I spiralled through
An organic 'Time Funnel'
Emerging to the sound of cheers?!
Finding over fifty people round me in a huddle

The Oak Tree had grown, lived and died
And what remained was just the bark outside
(See similar photos)

I said, "My goodness me!
What happened there?
Where am I now and what's the year?
Some soul approached me 'bout forty one
Saying, "We've been waiting for you
And I'm your hundredth generation!"

Mute with horror and somewhat annoyed
The spirit reassured me
And I became overjoyed
I said, "I thought the human race
Would all be dead!"
They said, "Oh no. They listened to you and acted instead"
Save the World Club and your friends made history
You saved the Earth, so you saved me

I asked them, "Tell me 'bout your world some?"
They said, "We communicate by poem and song
And as you only have eight minutes
And twenty six seconds
That doesn't leave us long"
They told me, "Many worthy people
Had to sacrifice, stand up and say
To think and act in your radical new way
To collect, conserve and re-circulate
To save the world before it was too late
Millions joined you, and the media loved you
But it took decades to change and educate

Selling weapons and waging war

Doesn't happen any more
A Basic Income feeds the poor
And no one needs to starve no more
Although the seas have risen sixty meters
And much of what you knew's beneath us
All transport now is electro-magnetic
Using fossil fuels is seen as barbaric"

I asked, "Have you mastered the constellations?"
They said, "Oh no. We're busy cleaning radiation
As nuclear power plants were by the coast
Decommissioning cost the most
AI (Artificial Intelligence) had its day
But sustainability is now our way
We live with nature organically
Wealth is universal thankfully
We love humour, caring and art
For we weigh our wealth
By contents of hearts"

Then when my time was almost through
They said, "We know the people of your time
Won't believe you
So tell them the signs are already there
That facts are facts scientifically clear"
They said, "Show the flooded maps
That were printed in the 'The Sun'
And keep on writing and telling everyone"

Then instantly I was back
I staggered dumbfound up the track
Back to good old twenty-twenty
Where I hugged my family plenty
So I thanked the spirit for his care

Then he swore that he'd protect me
In the last place I'd think
That he would find me there.

Angel of the Hood

Paul Cockle,
Is a man of his word,
A really good human,
If you haven't heard.

A master carpenter,
And Chessington's heart,
My long lost brother,
Too long been apart.

He's the spirit of Robin Hood,
His 'Maid Marion' knows,
He really does good,
Wherever he goes.

And with all his merry friends,
He does even more good,
Rescuing and giving free food,
With his 'Angels of the Hood'.

During the lockdown,
When many didn't know what to do,
He, Friar Tuck, Will Scarlet and Marion too,
Helped Save the World Club,
Rescue good food to give to you.

Did you eat when you were hungry,

Because of this man?
Did you drink when you were thirsty,
Because of this man?
Did you find that he smiled and listened,
And acted and understands?

For this is a man,
Who photos the moon and stars,
Who is wise and knows who you are.
So with your cheeky smile and winks,
And a cock of your hat,
From 'Zorro' to 'Robin',
I say thank you for that.

And I say, may you and your folk,
Get merry and joke,
To celebrate your life,
And your beautiful wife,
Saying thank you to you,
The great Paul Cockle,
Nay! 'Robin Hood',
The saviour of my life.

Each Moment We Had

In the name of the rain
And the clouds in the sky
I swear by my pain
That my tears will never dry

I completely fell apart
Leaving a sad and broken heart
But in my grief
I recalled your strength of belief
So all the memories we shared
Will always be there

For I was yours and you were mine
And I'll love you beyond the time
When the stars will cease to shine

In good times and bad
Whether we were happy or sad
I'll never forget
Your soul, your spirit, your love
And all that bloomed
From the miracle of how we met
And each moment we had.

An Ode to Simon J Johnson

Dedicated to Simon J Johnson who tragically passed away in November 2017. Simon was Tariq's friend and song-writing partner and is missed to this day.

My late friend and lyricist Simon
Had a heart like a Diamond

His humour was dark as coal
But he had a Golden soul

I miss him so much
That I could die
And every day
All I do is cry

You went to early
My dear friend
But I will meet you
In the end

So I hope that
With this verse
I tried to be
As clever and as kind
As you were to me.

Happy Day

Who, what, where and when?
Who, what, why and how?

If you've got an idea,
And you've got a vision,
If you've got a concept,
And you've got a mission,
You can trade in something new,
And make some money for me and you…

Then no more duckin' and divin',
No more wheelin' and dealin',
No more scrimping and saving,
No more commuting or slaving,
No more bills to pay, hey, hey,
It'll be a Happy Day, hey, hey.

If you've lost your job,
Or your income has fallen,
If your money's all gone,
And you've got a problem,
You can build your enterprise,
And open up Alan Sugars' eyes,

Then no more duckin' and divin',
No more wheelin' and dealin',
No more scrimping and saving,

No more commuting or slaving,
No more bills to pay, hey, hey
It'll be a Happy Day, hey, hey

If you've got a product,
And you've got a market,
If you've got a service,
And you've got a target,
You can build your enterprise,
And give Richard Branson a big surprise,

Then there'll be no Credit Card bills,
You could do anything,
You could be anything,
No more bills to pay,
It'll be a Happy Day.
It'll be a Happy Day.

Let's Love

Verse 1
Let's plan,
Let's share together,
We can,
Really work together,
Let's live,
Let's give,
Let's love.

Verse 2
Let's spend,
Let's earn together,
Let's lend,
Let's learn together,
Let's live,
Let's give,
Let's love.

Bridge:
Help each other,
Every day,
Find new ways,
To survive,
(And to thrive).

Verse 3

Let's eat,
Let's drink together,
Let's meet,
Let's think together,
Let's live,
Let's give,
Let's love.

(We need you, you, you.)

Don't You Judge

I say hey!
What you looking at man?,
Am I all of the things,
You don't understand,
I say hey, hey, hey,
Don't you judge me!

Don't make assumptions,
By what I wear,
Look beneath,
For the person there.
There is good and bad,
In every one,
Don't you know?

Don't you class me,
As being just black or white,
I don't conform,
To your stereotype.
We don't need to discriminate,
We just need to communicate.

I say hey,
What you looking at girl?
Am I all of the things,
You hate in the world?
I say hey, hey, hey,

Don't you judge me!

I'm not worried,
About the way I walk,
Or not ashamed,
By the way I talk.
It's your condescending platitudes,
That's the problem here,
I don't need your damn attitudes!

You don't see,
What's really here,
Try and look,
Beyond your fears.
My colour skin,
Doesn't define my worth,
I don't have to prove,
My place on Earth.

I said hey,
What you looking at boy?
Am I all of the things,
You want to destroy?
I say hey, hey, hey,
Don't you judge me!

Why do I feel,
Like a refugee?
Only fleeing,
Death and tyranny.
They're the victims,
Of futile wars,
Terror, famines',
Not of their cause.

They don't want,
Handouts,
Or charity,
But let me tell you,
Some reality.
They don't want,
To be misconstrued,
They want to earn,
Just like you!

I said hey,
What you thinking man?
I said hey,
What you thinking girl?
I said hey,
What you thinking boy?
Are WE all of the things,
You want to destroy?

I said hey, hey, hey,
Don't you judge me!

Super Human

You make me feel,
Super Human,
You make me feel,
Feel loved,
You make me feel,
Super Human,
Super, Duper Human!

Verse 1
You're my reflection,
My help and guide,
I always want you,
By my side,
You're my partner,
My closest friend,
To the end, to the end,

Verse 2
My dreams were met when,
I found you,
My path was set when,
You loved me too,
My loneliness has,
Flown away,
Now I know
Our love will grow,

You make me feel,
Super Human,
You make me feel,
Feel loved,
You make me feel,
Super Human,
Super, Duper Human!

Verse 3

When I'm with you,
I feel complete,
When I'm sour,
You make me sweet,
I've found my treasure,
My priceless friend,
To the end,
To the end.

Bridge

You are my destiny,
You find the best in me,
You are my one de – sire,
You give me everything,
You make my spirit sing,
You set my soul on fire,

You make me feel,
Super Human,
You make me feel,
Feel loved,
You make me feel,
Super Human,
Super, Duper Human!

I love you,
Yes I do....

Van Can

to the tune of 'Downtown' by Petula Clark

Our van broke down,
With the strain of lockdown,
To deliver rescued food. *(res-cue)*
We feed the poor and homeless,
Single mums and the disabled too. *(rescue)*

We lost our van, we're in a fix,
To get the food to you.
Hungry people round the world,
Are just like me and you,
Surviving each day...

Children can eat,
Making ends meet.

Save the World Club,
Rescues good food for you,
Save the World Club,
Delivers good food to you,
You can help us,
Not asking much from you,
Now, now!
(Donate now, now)

If you're feeling helpless,
And you want to do good,

Well you can help us now,
Now, now.

You can make a donation,
Really help us out,
So we don't feel so down,
Down, down.

We need a van to rescue food,
For those self isolating.
Our van broke down,
We raised some funds,
But there are hungry waiting,
For us to come by...

Children can eat,
Making ends meet.

Save the World Club,
Rescues good food for you,
Save the World Club,
Delivers good food to you,
You can help us,
Not asking much from you,
Now, now!
(Donate now, now)

Please can you help me?

Verse 1
I've got an idea,
And I've got a vision,
I've got a concept,
And I've got a mission.

Save the World Club charity,
Rescues food for you and me,

(Chorus)
So the kids won't be hungry,
So the poor won't be thirsty,
Oh please won't you help me?...

Verse 2
Our van broke down,
And we need a new one,
To rescue more food,
And do something human.
We need ten thousand pounds,
For a van to run around...

(Chorus)
So the kids won't be hungry,
So the poor won't be thirsty,
Oh please won't you help me?...

Outro

So the kids won't be hungry,
So the poor won't be thirsty,
Oh please can you help me?
Oh please can you help me?

NHS Thank You Song

We thank you,
We're always thinking of you,
We thank you,
For everything you do,
Do, do,
Do, do

Verse 1
NHS we love you,
Nurses we love you,
Doctors we love you,
Clinicians we love you.

We thank you,
We're always thinking of you,
We thank you,
For everything you do,
Do, do,
Do, do

Verse 2
New Malden we thank you,
Kingston we thank you,
London we th-a-nk you,
UK we th-a-nk you.

We thank you,
We're always thinking of you,
We thank you,
For everything you do,
Do, do,
Do, do

Bridge:
You are the ones,
Who give us hope,
Serving those,
Who cannot cope,
Helping those without any-thing,
Saving lives and sur-vi-ving.

-     *Chorus to infinity and beyond!*   -

Maggie Pound Is So Very Sound

Maggie Pound is so very sound,
Both generous and kind.
When you meet,
And make a friend of her,
A better type you'll never find.

She's so caring,
And helps the poor,
A really sweet character,
That you can adore.

A lover of animals and nature,
Her spark and passion,
Is what makes her,
And I'm very glad to say,
Have a wonderful Birthday.

For even if forty is the new seventy,
And fifty the new eighty ....
Age does not fade you.

For your spirit and drive,
Keeps you young and alive,
And it takes alot to faze you.

So Happy Birthday Maggie Pound,
May you always stay,
Safe and sound.
Have a really gorgeous day,
And thanks for calling us around.

Changing My Mind

Verse 1
I've been cruel,
I've been kind,
Been ahead and,
Been behind.
Been alone,
Been in love,
Been below and,
Been above.

I've been changing my mind,
I've been changing my mind.

Verse 2
I've been up,
I've been down,
I've been through and,
I've been round.
I've been left,
I've been right,
I've been weak and,
I've felt might.

I've been changing my mind,
I've been changing my mind.

Bridge

Now nothing ever stays the same,
Our lives are bound to change,
I'm sure it's all for the good
I'm sure it's all as it,
Should be,
How it should be.

Verse 3
I've been rich,
I've been poor,
I've been many things before.
I've been sane,
I've been mad,
With the life that,
I have had.

I've been changing my mind,
I've been changing my mind.

The Sweetness of Your Smile

In the…
Deepest darkest of the night,
Your love,
Shines like light.
Your love,
Brings me,
Loving every day,
Your love,
Is so bright.

(Chorus)
The sweetness of your smile,
Can make me walk miles,
Remembering your smile,
Can make me run miles,
With the sweetness of your smile,
I can cycle for miles.
'Cause it's the …
Sweetness of your sm – ii- iii - le,
The sweetness of your sm – ii- iii – le.

Verse 2
When I'm …
Blue and feeling down,
I think,

Of you.
If you,
Were to,
Somehow go away,
I'd die,
Without you.

(Chorus)

The sweetness of your smile,
Can make me walk miles.
Remembering your smile,
Can make me run miles.
With the sweetness of your smile,
I can cycle for miles.
'Cause it's the ...
Sweetness of your sm – ii- iii - le,
The sweetness of your sm – ii- iii – le.

It's Christmas Time

It's Christmas time,
We're feeling fine,
It's Christmas time,
You're feeling fine.
Peace and love around the Earth,
A season filled with joy and mirth,
Christmas food and drink,
Does it make you think?
Maybe…

Santa's flying,
Children sighing,
Chimney climbing,
Present hiding,
The Christmas stocking's filled with glee,
There's presents round the Christmas tree,
Bless our food and drink,
Does it make you think?
Maybe…

Snowflakes swirling,
Candles burning,
Tinsel glitters,
Cold is bitter,
Sliding down an icy hill,
The air is crisp and sweet and chill,
Snowmen freezing in the night,

Trees and ground are brilliant white,
Around you...

Rudolph's prancing,
Santa's dancing,
Windows frosting,
Dinners roasting,
Waiting for a big surprise,
Love is gleaming in their eyes,
Fridges over flow,
While there's sleet and snow,
Outside...

Carol singing,
Presents glistening,
Children smiling,
Hearts are shining,
Remember who was born today,
The Prince of Peace and loving ways,
Meeting with your friends,
Loneliness will end,
All things…
Christmas dinner,
Is a winner,
With forgiveness and hope,
Some how we will cope,
Millions smile and stop being sad,
And travel home to mum and dad,
Christmas cards displayed,
The table's all been laid,
For you…

It's Christmas time,
We're feeling fine,

It's Christmas time,
You're feeling fine,
Peace and love on the Earth,
A season for some joy and mirth,
Christmas food and drink,
Does it make you think?
Maybe…

Fooling Around With You

as sung by Dr Tariq Shabbeer before Kingston Council's annual Budget Meeting, March 2020

Kingston,
What you gonna do?
I am sick and tired of
fooling around with you.

The Earth is getting warmer,
The seas are getting high,
You better go Green or
we all will die.

Planes and cars and lorries
are smogging up our air,
Our economic system
really doesn't care.

Our habitats are dying,
All insects in decline,
No rhino, bees or pandas,
Now that's the bottom line.
The budgets for the "Fat Cats"
and nothing for the poor,
Your budget doesn't care
about people anymore.

We're calling on the Council
to cost up a better way,
To listen to the people,
And ACT on what they say.

ABOUT THE AUTHOR

Dr Tariq Shabbeer is 58 years young. Married for 30 years with two sons. Born and brought up in London of Pakistani heritage. Both Tariq's parents wrote poetry in Urdu and are MAs in English Literature. He has been a Green Party activist since 1990.

Tariq is an Oceanographer and PhD in Acid Rain. An environmentalist, singer, guitarist and songwriter of over 40 years. The four-month lockdown gave him time to explore and express himself through poetry and song composition.

The pandemic also resulted in the loss of a secure income. Tariq loves helping vulnerable people, feeding the hungry and spends a lot of time helping others - often at a cost to himself and family.

Tariq hopes that this collection of original poems, prose and songs will sow the seeds of change needed to bring about REAL world peace soon, rather than in a thousand years' time (as in the Damson Spirit). But does humankind have that long?

All profits from the sale of this material will fund charitable works through the Save the World Club charity, Kingston Environment Centre and other ecological, social and economic regeneration projects helping all to cope with and recover from the effects of lockdown and the pandemic. Tariq says:

"May these words reach your heart
Whether you are near or far apart
Locally, regionally or internationally
And for a thousand years to come".
......

Tariq

7th Nov 2020 1.30 am

(Composed at the Kingston Environment Centre)

Printed in Poland
by Amazon Fulfillment
Poland Sp. z o.o., Wrocław